# Changes

## by David McCoy

Orlando   Boston   Dallas   Chicago   San Diego

Visit *The Learning Site!*

**www.harcourtschool.com**

Every living thing changes. You know that
people go through stages in their lives. First, they
are babies. They grow and become children, and
then teenagers. Finally, they become adults.

Animals go through changes in their lives, too.
They also start small and become big.

In this book you will learn about four animals.
You will see how they change from stage to stage.

# THE DRAGONFLY

### Stage 1—Egg

A dragonfly must lay her eggs in water. Some dragonflies just drop their eggs into the water. Others attach their eggs to water plants.

### Stage 2—Nymph

A dragonfly nymph hatches from an egg. The nymph looks like a worm. It lives underwater for one to three years, changing slowly. When the nymph has changed completely, it crawls out of the water for good. It has become an adult dragonfly.

### Stage 3—Adult

An adult dragonfly has two pairs of wings. It can fly as soon as its wings dry.

A dragonfly has large compound eyes. The eyes are at the top of its head. It's impossible to sneak up on a dragonfly. It glances all around itself while flying. It can see below, above, behind, and sideways! The dragonfly's eyes and wings help it catch insects in the air.

Most of a dragonfly's life is spent as a nymph. Dragonflies live as adults for only a short time. They live long enough to mate. Female dragonflies live long enough to lay eggs.

Dragonflies eat huge numbers of mosquitoes and other small insects. Dragonflies live near ponds, streams, rivers, and lakes. They are born in these places. Mosquitoes are born and live near these places, too. They provide plenty of food for the dragonflies.

Some dragonflies fly away from the place they were born. Dragonflies can fly as fast as 35 miles an hour. They can fly far, too. Dragonflies have been found on ships 200 miles out at sea.

# FROG

### Stage 1—Egg

Like dragonflies, frogs return to the water to lay their eggs. The eggs are surrounded by jelly. The jelly protects the eggs from harm. It helps the eggs float in the water and keeps the eggs from drying out. The female frog lays thousands of eggs. Few live. Many get eaten by fish.

### Stage 2—Tadpole

After a few days in the water, the frog egg begins to change. It starts to become a tadpole. A head and tail begin to develop.

Then the jelly that surrounds the eggs turns into liquid. Tadpoles hatch! For a few days, a tadpole eats what is left of the yolk from its egg. Later, the little tadpole gets food from the pond water it lives in.

About seven weeks after it hatches, a tadpole begins to grow its back legs. About twelve to fourteen weeks after hatching, the tadpole is not quite an adult frog. It is sometimes called a froglet. It has both front and back legs. It no longer has a tail. The tail has become part of its body.

### Stage 3—Adult

At sixteen weeks, what is now a small frog leaves the water. The frog hops off to its new life on land. Frogs eat insects and spiders. The frog catches them with its long tongue.

On warm spring nights, you can sometimes hear one bullfrog begin croaking. The noise seems to be contagious, and the other frogs join in.

Most frogs live near fresh water, where they can find food and escape from danger. Water must be in the prescription because they need to keep their moist skins from drying out.

# PEAFOWL

### Stage 1—Egg

A female is called a peahen. She may lay from three to twelve eggs. Most lay from four to six eggs. The eggs are usually laid two days apart. Peafowl eggs take about a month to hatch.

### Stage 2—Chick

When a peachick hatches, it is wet. In a very short time, its feathers dry. When a peachick is not even one day old, it can eat, drink, and even walk on its own! A peachick is born with flight feathers. It can fly by the time it is just one week old.

### Stage 3—Adult

Peafowl live in small groups called flocks. Each flock is made up of one peacock and four or five peahens. Peafowl build their nests in tree branches near or on the ground.

A peacock is about as big as a turkey. The peacock, not the peahen, has the famous long blue and green feathers. The feathers, called a train, grow on the peacock's back above its tail.

The peacock can fan out his train. He raises and spreads out the feathers. He does this to get the peahen's attention.

The peacock also fans out his long feathers to let other peacocks know he is there. He wants them to stay away. The showy peacock makes them look at him. That way they may not notice the peahen and peachicks.

Most peafowl come from Asia. They are so beautiful they were taken to many other places. You can see them in zoos and some parks and gardens.

Peafowl eat many kinds of food. They eat berries, flowers, seeds, insects, worms, and sometimes snakes.

# KANGAROO

## Stage 1—Birth

Kangaroos are different from other animals.
Kangaroo babies develop inside the mother's body
for only a very short time. A mother kangaroo
gives birth to one baby at a time. When born, the
pink, hairless kangaroo baby is less than 1 inch
long. It weighs less than an ounce.

When it is born, the tiny kangaroo baby's eyes,
ears, and hind legs have not yet developed. It grabs
its mother's fur and slowly climbs into her pouch.
Once in the pouch, the baby attaches itself to its
mother and starts to nurse.

## Stage 2—Joey

The baby continues to grow there for about six months or so. It develops its eyes, ears, and hind legs. By the end of this period, the baby kangaroo is covered in fur like its mother. It is now called a joey. It is ready to come out of the pouch and enter the outside world.

The joey stays with its mother even after it has "moved out" of her pouch. For a few months, the joey will put its head inside the pouch to nurse. Many a joey has tried to climb in when it longed for the comfort of its mother's pouch.

### Stage 3—Adult

Some adult male kangaroos can be as big as 8 feet tall. They can weigh 150 pounds. Female kangaroos are a little smaller.

The kangaroo has a rather small head for its body. A kangaroo has short front legs that it uses like arms. Kangaroos have big, strong hind legs that they use to jump large distances. Their long, thick tails help them keep their balance.

There are more than fifty kinds of kangaroos, of different sizes. In Australia, the antelope kangaroo lives in grassy areas. The gray kangaroo lives in forests. The red kangaroo lives in deserts and dry areas. Kangaroos eat grasses and other plants. Besides Australia, kangaroos live in New Guinea and Tasmania, as well as on some nearby islands. Some were taken to New Zealand.

Kangaroos live alone or in small groups. Kangaroos also get together in large groups called mobs. Mobs can have from fifty to several hundred members.

## Glossary

**flock**    a group of peafowl

**froglet**    the stage between a tadpole and an adult frog

**joey**    a young kangaroo

**mob**    a group of kangaroos

**nymph**    the larva stage of a dragonfly

**peacock**    a male peafowl

**peahen**    a female peafowl

**tadpole**    a baby frog that lives in the water

**train**    an adult peacock's long showy feathers